LIVES TURNED UPSIDE DOWN

BY JIM HUBBARD

Founder of Shooting Back

HOMELESS CHILDREN IN THEIR OWN WORDS AND PHOTOGRAPHS

SIMON & SCHUSTER BOOKS FOR YOUNG READERS
An imprint of Simon & Schuster Children's Publishing Division
1230 Avenue of the Americas, New York, New York 10020
Copyright © 1996 by Jim Hubbard
SIMON & SCHUSTER BOOKS FOR YOUNG READERS is a trademark of Simon & Schuster.
Book design by Paul Zakris
The text for this book is set in 13–point Nofret
Printed and bound in the United States of America
First Edition
10 9 8 7 6 5 4 3 2 1
ISBN 0–689–80649–3
CIP data for this data book is available from the Library of Congress

To all the young people who are homeless
and in memory of my first-born daughter,
Brijin Marie Hubbard

ACKNOWLEDGEMENTS

Thanks to :

Almighty God; my daughters, Priya and Hanna Hubbard; Sherry Hubbard; Lois Hubbard; the Sunlight Mission Church and its staff, Sean Vincent Levy and his wife, Sharon Levy, pastors Willa and Kenny Feldman; The Prudential Foundation and Mary Puryear; The *Los Angeles Times* and staffers Larry Armstrong, Judith Dugan, Carolyn Cole, and Fred Sweets; Copley Newspapers and staffers Andrea Roth and Josh Grossberg; LA Bookstore in Santa Monica, California; National Camera Exchange in Minneapolis; Pro Ex in Minneapolis; Red; Vicki Payzant; Summerfield Suites and Paul Parker and Chris Gebbert; Anne Edelstein, literary agent; David Gale, Michael Conathan, and Paul Zakris at Simon & Schuster Books for Young Readers; *bonne viande*, Starbucks Coffee, and Borders Book Shop at Calhoun Square in Minneapolis; Pascale Ferron Philbert; Brian Heflin, Jr., and his family; Sarah Lewis and her family; Christina Coito and her family; and Lennie and his family.

FOREWORD

Homelessness is a recurring disaster in the United States, affecting millions of people, including children. Young people who are homeless find their lives turned upside down: moving a lot, losing touch with friends, lacking privacy. Here, in their own words and pictures, are the stories of two girls and two boys who know this reality firsthand. Either presently or recently homeless, these four children have experienced the turmoil of not having a permanent place to call home.

In the early 1980s, as a documentary photojournalist working for United Press International (UPI), I began photographing some of the growing number of homeless people. I learned that the reasons leading to their homelessness were as varied as the people themselves. Through the people I met, I became sensitive to the struggles many homeless youngsters face. I agonized over how to help these young and innocent victims of our national social disgrace.

I decided to offer some of these children, who had lots of time and little to do, the opportunity to learn photography. In 1989 I started a program called Shooting Back. The idea behind the program was simple: Give these children a chance to document their own lives through photography. Exhibits of their pictures and narratives in

"OR THE KIDS"
©1993
COVARRUBIAS, RUBEN ACEVES,
UVAL, & TORI GOLDSMITH

galleries and other settings would educate the public about the issues these children face daily. The first show, by homeless children in and around Washington, D.C., has traveled around the world for over five years. It was also published in a book called *Shooting Back: A Photographic View of Life by Homeless Children*. President Bill Clinton and Hillary Rodham Clinton have honored the work by calling it one of the most vital creative projects in America.

Shooting Back also completed a second project, with Native American youths. Those photographs and commentaries were published in a book called *Shooting Back from the Reservation*.

So far, more than two hundred projects modeled after Shooting Back have been started around the world. Several of the graduates of the Shooting Back programs have gone on to form their own photographic businesses, and some of them have worked on other photographic projects in the United States and Europe.

For *Lives Turned Upside Down*, I worked with four children who learned photography quickly and allowed me to interview them so they could share their views of their world.

We see through the lives of these four youngsters that the term *homeless* is an oversimplification for a large number of people who are without permanent homes. Sarah Lewis, age ten, and Christina Coito, age nine, live at the Sunlight Mission Church in Santa Monica, Calif–

ornia. These two dynamic and spirited girls live in a shelter with over fifty other homeless people. Lennie, age twelve, and his family have lived in their car, in parks, and in abandoned buildings. He is not homeless now, but he and his family move frequently in order to find work. Brian Heflin, age nine, lives in Alexandria, Virginia. When he and his family lived in

a shelter, his two older brothers participated in the first Shooting Back project. Brian's family lives in a house now, but they can't afford to pay for electricity.

An ironic event happened while working on this book. Someone broke into my car and stole two bags containing all the photos that Christina and Sarah had taken, along with the negatives, some cameras, and my personal belongings. When the husband and wife ministerial team at the Sunlight Mission Church heard about the theft, Pastor Willa said, "You watch what the Lord does with this. We are going to pray about this tonight."

The next day, a woman in Los Angeles who had found my checkbook directed me to a park some fifteen miles from where the theft had taken place, where she had seen photographs strewn all over the sidewalk. There I met Red, who reached into his shopping cart and pulled out one of my business cards. He said he had found the items in a garbage bag and dropped them into a nearby mailbox. I went to the nearest post office to start the process of trying to retrieve the children's pictures and negatives. One day, the stolen items may be returned. How ironic, that homeless children spend days photographing their lives for this book, and a homeless man fifteen miles away attempts to return them to us. Pastor Willa's take on this was expressed when she said, "The Lord works in mysterious ways."

—*Jim Hubbard*
<small>September 1996</small>

SARAH LEWIS

Age 10, Santa Monica, California

I'm not really homeless, because I have a place to live. I live in the Sunlight Mission Church with my brother, Kevin, and my mother. We don't have a shopping cart like real homeless people. They have to put all of their stuff in the cart and push it around all day and stay under trees and under bridges and hide. They have their stuff stolen from them. Sure, people do sometimes steal from other people, even at the Sunlight Mission Church, but it is still a nice place to live.

Christina is my best friend. I have a lot of friends at the shelter and at school, but I don't have neighbors. Neighbors are when you have your own place and people live next door. Here I just have friends.

Some people say that we actually are more than friends in the mission. We are like a family. Even Pastor Kenny says that. It's funny, because we play and even fight like a real family. My brother, Kevin, gets in play fights and maybe even real ones sometimes, but I don't like fights. Me and Kevin get along real well and he is one of my best friends. He gets moody sometimes and wants to be alone, but I do, too, sometimes.

Me and Kevin and my mother have been living in the mission for several months. My dad lives in Washington state. We used to all live in a house together, and that was good, but things didn't work out, and my parents split up. Actually, I didn't like living with my dad so

much. He was too strict and made me do too many things. Sometimes he was mean. I am glad to be living with my mom and my brother.

Life in the shelter is pretty good and I usually have fun, but sometimes it is bor–ing. I can't bring my friends home from school and it is sometimes hard to tell other people that I live in the Sunlight Mission Church. Other kids in school sometimes make fun of me.

I brought the camera to my school to show what it is like. Some of the kids at school said it was stupid to be in a dumb homeless book, and I felt really embar–rassed and sad. When I left school with Christina, I covered my head with my jack–et. I didn't want to take any more pictures or be in a dumb homeless book because I am not homeless. When I got to the mission I started feeling okay again. I decided I wanted to take more pictures for the book and show how I play and show my friends for the book. It's okay now.

Some of the other kids in school have stayed at the shelter and they are the ones who say the worst stuff and embarrass us. They say it is awful and it has cockroaches and you have to go to church all the time. Sure there are some cockroaches, and I have even seen them crawling on the chairs in church, but we have to be here and I'm not afraid of them. When we have a house of our own, there won't be any cockroaches.

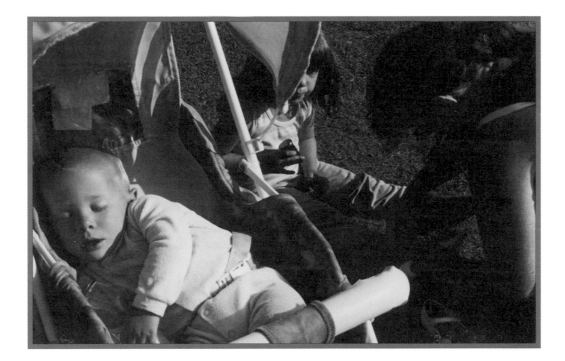

Everyone has to be out of the shelter from one to four in the after–noon unless they are sick or it is raining. During lockout we can go to the park or the beach or PAL (the recreation center next to the park).

Since the people from the shelter have to spend so many hours each day outside, sometimes it gets awfully boring. We just have to find things to do until the shelter lets us back in. Some of the moms and their little kids stay in the park all the time because the little ones aren't in school yet. I feel bad for some of the mothers with little kids, because they have to stay there so long, and the kids cry and stuff.

Christina and I come back to the shelter after lockout and enter through the alley, where there is a huge fence with wire at the top and a sign that says DANGER: NO TRESPASSING. We can play on the bars

and do flips and swing. Besides swinging and jumping, I like to draw and make up stories and make up my own dances and listen to music. I also like to read a lot.

When we used to have a house, I had my own room and friends could come over and play. Then we had to leave and me and my mom and brother had to find other places to live and we finally moved here, to the Sunlight Mission Church. I miss having my own room and privacy. In a shelter we don't have much privacy, but we aren't homeless, either.

The president should have homes and jobs for everybody and nobody should have to be on the street with a shopping cart, and I would tell him this if I met him.

I dream about living in a house again. There will be big rooms inside, one for me, one for Kevin, and one for my mom. It will be white or yellow and there will be a white fence in front and we will have a dog. There will be a swimming pool for the hot days and we can bring all of our friends over. I will invite Christina over first if I still know where she is. I'm afraid I will never see my friends again when we leave here or when they leave.

My room will have a big closet and the bed will have a cover over it like you see the rich people have in the movies. My bed will have four pillows and soft sheets like silk.

We will be able to come and go as we please because there won't be any lockout like at the Sunlight Mission Church. My mom and Kevin and me will get along really well and my mother will have a good job and we will have lots of money and won't have to move again for a long time. We will have a home of our own.

CHRISTINA COITO

Age 9, Santa Monica, California

Life at the Sunlight Mission Church is pretty good, but it can be hard, too. It is better than living in a car like we did for lots of nights. When you live in a car, it's very crowded and it's hard to find places to put all your stuff. Me and my brother, Jeremy, slept in the back and my mom and Willie slept in the front. (Willie is not my real dad, but he treats me real well.) It was hard to sleep sometimes and noisy and even scary at times. Whenever someone coughed or snored, I would wake up and sometimes it was hard to get back to sleep. When I see people sleeping on the street I feel bad for them, because I know how hard it is to sleep even on a softer car seat. At least in the Sunlight Mission Church there are beds and sofas.

Only a few people know I live in the shelter. It's okay but sometimes hard. We all have to do our share of the work. We have chores to do, and if we don't do our share, then we can get kicked out. It's not mean there, though. People are pretty nice. It's sad when someone has to leave or if someone steals from someone else. That has happened, and the person had to leave.

Living at the shelter, we have to go to church four times a week unless we are sick. It's important. I like church most of the time. We have been dedicated in the church. Pastor Kenny gave us certificates.

Some of my friends wonder how we can go to church so many times in a week. It is a lot, but I know someone who stayed in another

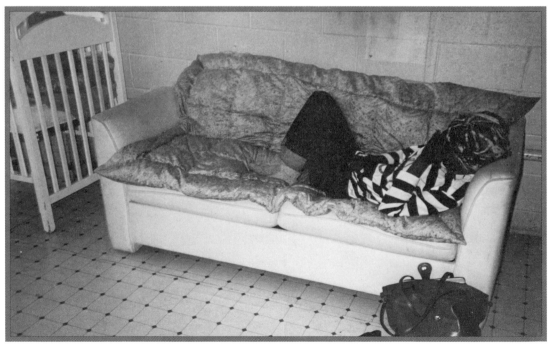

shelter somewhere in Los Angeles and they had to go to church every day and study the Bible all the time and memorize it.

Sometimes I fall asleep in church. It's hard not to, because we have to listen to all the words that the pastor says four times a week. Pastor Kenny has told us to sleep when it is bedtime, and not during church. Sarah falls asleep in church, too. It's funny, because Sarah plays tambourine when the music is playing during the church service. Maybe she is tired after she plays the tambourine.

Sarah is one of my best friends. She is a fun friend, but she is sometimes sad and gets mad at me. She told me that we are not homeless, because we live in the Sunlight Mission Church. I know we are homeless. We will not be able to stay in the shelter forever. We may have to go to another shelter or live in our car again or even in the park. Being homeless is not any fun. No one should have to live in the street or in a car or in a park.

Sarah and I do lots of things together. We both go to the Will Rogers School now and we like it. We walk there and back together. Sometimes we walk with our other friends who stay at the mission and go to school with us. We have lots of fun together and laugh and play and talk about our dreams together.

Sometimes we talk about what our own houses will be like. My house will be big, really big, with a three-car garage and a swimming pool and sundeck and a place to Rollerblade and skateboard. Inside there will be at least five bedrooms for us and all our stuff. I once dreamed about being in a new house with my family, and Sarah and Kevin were there. Something in the dream scared me, but I don't remember what. Dreams are fun but scary, too.

I hope we have our own place someday. We are homeless but we have a place to stay now, and that's good. I like my friends here and will be really sad if they leave or I leave. Some of my friends have had to leave and I have been really sad that I might never see them again. One of my friends has a dad who is in prison, and some of the people here have been in trouble with the police. Sometimes kids have been taken away from their mothers and fathers because of drugs or something like that, and they are so happy when they get back together.

My mother, Jeremy, and Willie sometimes get upset that we have to be in a shelter, and I know they want us to have our own place. I want us to have our own house, and we will someday, but right now being in the mission is better than living in the car.

LENNIE

Age 12, Minneapolis, Minnesota

My life is lots of fun, but it is hard to be moving a lot and lose touch with my friends. I have been to so many schools and met so many people. I guess my home is in Minneapolis because we spend a lot of time there, but we also stay in lots of other places. We are leaving for Oklahoma soon. We have lived in South Dakota, Oklahoma, and Minnesota, and even on reservations a few times. We move a lot.

My mother has told me we have to go where we can find work or get some money or stay with people we know. I know other kids who have to do this, too. I think that because we have to move around so much, I get to see many things that people who don't travel so much probably don't get to see.

Now there are gambling casinos on reservations, and we sometimes go there. The food is great and my mother tries to make lots of money for us. Sometimes she wins and sometimes she doesn't. She says that maybe someday she will strike it rich and we will buy a big home and a new car. I think that if we didn't have to travel so much, my mother would like to spend more time in the casino.

Most of the time I live with my mother and brothers and sisters, and once I lived with my aunt for a few months. I ran away two times but only for a little while. I was scared and missed my family. I met some nice kids, though.

We lived in our car many times and in parks and a few times in abandoned buildings. It is hard to stay in cars, because sometimes they are scary.

I am part Indian but we really don't have much contact with other Native Americans because we are never in one place for very long. We know some people on reservations and have some relatives there, but mostly we are around white people. I've gone to powwows and they are lots of fun. The kids dance and wear these really great clothes with feathers and beads.

I'm lucky because I have met people who are from many back-grounds, like Native Americans, Asian Americans, and African Americans. We lived for a while in St. Paul and I met some Hmong kids and hung out with them. The family of one of the kids sold veg-etables at a market every week. I liked going there, but I don't get to

see them now because we moved away.

I really want to have a big house someday and not have to move all the time. The house would be big and white and we would have a fence around it and a dog in the backyard.

I think I would like to be a photographer someday and show how people are and how they live, so other people could learn. I love to read and take pictures. I might even like to write, but pictures are more fun. I like to photograph houses, and cars, and boats, and kids, and costumes, and dream catchers, and things at powwows.

In the city there are things to photograph that you don't see in the country or on reservations, like a stop sign that had writing, maybe from a gang, all over it. We also saw a really weird truck with things all over it–it was cool but it was near where a young guy had just been murdered. Cities are scary sometimes because there are too many fights and gangs and drugs, and people drink too much. My mother says this is a problem for everyone.

Everyone should be able to have money and not have to sleep in cars and parks. They should have houses. Families are very important and should be able to stay together all the time. I met a woman with a dog, and all her things were in a shopping cart. She smiled at me and we talked, but I don't think she should have to always be out–side without a house.

BRIAN HEFLIN

Age 9, Alexandria, Virginia

It's finally my turn to take pictures and I love it. My brothers have been taking pictures since we lived in the Carpenter Shelter a few years ago. They took pictures of me, and now I can take pictures of them.

It was not great having to live in a shelter and be homeless. We had tiny little rooms and it was crowded and my mother had to bathe me in a sink that many other people used, too.

We live in a house now. It's nice and I have my own room, but we don't have any electricity. We haven't had any for a couple of weeks. My dad works real hard but he can't pay for it right now. We keep things in the freezer with ice we buy. My mom lights candles so we can see at night. She can light the stove with a match because it's a gas stove. My mom has a hard time because she fell down and was hurt bad. She has to use a cane, and she isn't able to do everything anymore.

I want you to see my brothers and sister because they are important to me. Chris and Norman share the downstairs. Chris is real smart but he got into trouble and has to go to court. He was charged with grand larceny because he stole someone's motorbike, but he says they loaned it to him. He is worried and I hope he is okay. My dad isn't Chris's real dad but he is his dad now. Norman is sometimes a little wild and can swing really high when we go to the playground.

My sister has her own room. She likes to play outside with her friends, and she loves our cat. Me and her play sometimes, too.

I like to do things with my brothers when they let me, even though they tease me, especially Norman. We take the King Street Metro into Washington. I love going to Washington because it's important and interesting and there are lots of people. The only problem is that I get scared on the train. In Washington there are so many things and people to take pictures of. There are lots of homeless people, too, who sit on the streets or ask people for money. We never had to do that. We could be homeless again, I think. I hope not.

I love taking pictures of people doing things. I want to be a professional photographer when I grow up. I roam my neighborhood taking pictures of everything, like my friends and my two cousins who live down the street.

We don't have much to do in our neighborhood, and it is sometimes very boring. I like to go to the playground or to McDonald's or Fuddruckers, where Chris works. We sometimes talk about how there was more to do when we were in the shelter. There were so many people around and we could have fun sometimes. Not all the time. There were lots of groups who would come there to help us, too, and bring us gifts at Christmas. I don't remember all of this, but my parents and brothers tell me about it. Chris and Norman say they had more fun at the shelter because it is boring at home.

I don't think people should be homeless, though, and everyone should be able to have electricity. My dad works hard and knows everything about computers, but he can't always pay for everything. He is going to teach me all about computers.

My life is like most of the other kid's on the block, but I don't think many of them have lived in a shelter and been homeless. My dad says that sometimes hard times make a better person out of you. He says I will be stronger for the things I have been through. I feel pretty strong now.

RESOURCES

National Student Campaign Against Hunger & Homelessness
11965 Venice Boulevard
Suite 408
Los Angeles, CA 90066
(310) 397-5270, extension 324, or (800) NOHUNGR

NSCAHH works with student organizations on campuses nationwide in an effort to end homelessness and hunger. They provide these groups with organizational assistance, information on starting new programs, and ideas for action and aid which students can put into effect in their own communities.

National Alliance to End Homelessness
1518 K Street, NW, Suite 206
Washington, DC 20005
Phone: (202) 638-1526
Fax: (202) 638-4664

A nonprofit membership organization, the National Alliance to End Homelessness brings groups together to fight for the common belief that homelessness is simply unacceptable in our society. They work toward overcoming homelessness by implementing programs that create housing and social services, and policy work to develop stronger legislation and resources.

National Network for Youth
1319 F Street, NW, Suite 401
Washington, DC 20004
Phone: (202) 783-7949
Internet: nn4youth@aol.com

The National Network for Youth was founded twenty years ago with the objective of finding a healthy means for young people to grow up safely and have the opportunity to lead productive lives. Through advocacy drives, a community youth development program, and numerous other activities, NNY helps tackle the obstacles children face in our society.

National Coalition for the Homeless
1612 K Street, NW, #1004
Washington, DC 20006
Phone: (202) 775-1322
Hotline: (202) 775-1372
Fax: (202) 775-1316

The National Coalition for the Homeless describes itself as an "advocacy network of homeless persons, activists, service providers, and others committed to a single goal–to *end* homelessness." NCH goes to great pains to keep homeless people directly involved in all of its work, using promotion, education, and grassroots organization to accomplish results.

Family Services America
11700 West Lake Park Drive
Milwaukee, WI 53224
Phone: (414) 359-1040
Information and referral: (800) 221-2681
Fax: (414) 359-1074

A network of smaller, local organizations, Family Services America connects groups that provide assistance to all kinds of families in crisis, including homeless families. FSA provides its members with consultation, an information center, and a united public policy office, among other services.

ABOUT SHOOTING BACK

Shooting Back seeks to engage and empower at-risk youth by offering them the tools for creative expression and self-discovery through mediums such as photography and related arts. Using exhibitions, events, and media exposure, Shooting Back strives to educate the public about poverty and its impact on young people.

Shooting Back offers information and technical assistance for groups interested in starting their own program. Please contact us at:

3010 Hennepin Avenue South, Suite 230
Minneapolis, MN 55408
(612) 825-0704